TROUBLE DOLLS

Jimmy Buffett & Savannah Jane Buffett

I L L U S T R A T E D   B Y   L A M B E R T   D A V I S

Voyager Books

Harcourt Brace & Company

SAN DIEGO   NEW YORK   LONDON

Requests for permission to make copies of any part of the work should
be mailed to: Permissions Department, Harcourt Brace & Company,
6277 Sea Harbor Drive, Orlando, Florida 32887-6777.

First Voyager Books edition 1997
Voyager Books is a registered trademark of Harcourt Brace & Company.

Library of Congress Cataloging-in-Publication Data
Buffett, Jimmy.
Trouble dolls/by Jimmy Buffett and Savannah Jane Buffett; illustrated by
Lambert Davis.—1st ed.
p. cm.
Summary: When her environmentalist father is lost in the Everglades,
Lizzie sets out to find him with the help of her dog, Spooner, and a family
of tiny Guatemalan trouble dolls.
ISBN 0-15-290790-4
ISBN 0-15-201501-9 (pbk.)
[1. Dolls—Fiction. 2. Magic—Fiction. 3. Everglades (Fla.)—Fiction.]
I. Buffett, Savannah Jane. II. Davis, Lambert, ill. III. Title.
PZ7.B894Tr   1991
[Fic]—dc20   89-34683

F E D C B A

Printed in Singapore

The illustrations in this book were done in acrylics on D'Arches 140-lb.
cold press watercolor paper.
The display type was hand-lettered by Brenda Walton, Sacramento,
California.
The text type was set in Garamond #3 by Thompson Type, San Diego,
California.
Color separations were made by Bright Arts Ltd., Singapore.
Printed and bound by Tien Wah Press, Singapore
This book was printed on Leykam recycled paper, which contains more than
20 percent postconsumer waste and has a total recycled content of at least 50
percent.
Production supervision by Warren Wallerstein and Ginger Boyer
Designed by Michael Farmer

Children, see what you can see.
—J.B. and S.J.B.

To courage, adventure, and to saving the Everglades
—L.D.

LIZZY RHINEHART watched the sun sink into Florida Bay.

Her father called her the Princess of the Tidal Flats, and her royal barge was a little skiff he had built for her eighth birthday. She had christened it the *Parakeet.* Spooner, her golden retriever and first mate, was on the bow stretching into the wind, smelling the approaching land. A blue macaw parrot soared overhead.

Lizzy drove her boat with the sure hand of a cautious captain and watched for the green flash when the sun slipped over the horizon. But today it did not show, and instinctively she turned toward the darkening sky in the east.

A falling star plummeted to the sea. Before it had burned out, Lizzy was organizing her wish. She knew how to pack several wishes into one.

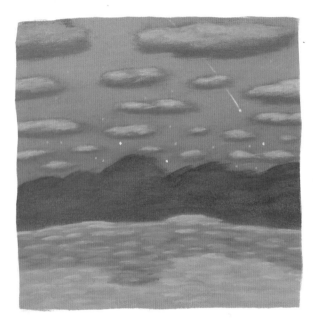

"*I wish for my father to return home safely; since my mother is in heaven and can't be with us, I wish her happiness; and I wish that maybe when my father gets home, he will help me with my math homework.*" At nine, Lizzy was very independent, but she always worried when her father, Michael Rhinehart, went away.

Tonight her father was flying home after a two-week project in the Everglades looking for panthers. He was a famous environmentalist and pilot who traveled the world trying to convince people everywhere that if we don't take better care of our Earth, we will see it change dangerously for the worse. Lizzy's mother had been killed in an avalanche in the Andes mountains of Peru when Lizzy was just a baby, and the little girl had been raised by her father and Mrs. Sweep, an old Seminole Indian.

Spooner began to bark. The trade winds were blowing delicious aromas from the kitchen, where Mrs. Sweep was cooking a homecoming meal. Lizzy tied up her boat, and she and Spooner headed for the house.

She hightailed it into the kitchen and snitched a piece of Bimini bread from the table, tossing half to Spooner. She knew she had to hurry; soon her father's seaplane would land behind the house. She was his official greeter and loved to meet him in the *Parakeet* to tow his plane to its mooring in the canal.

Lizzy called to Mrs. Sweep. There was no answer, which was odd, but then she saw her on the phone. Mrs. Sweep turned, and the look on her face told Lizzy something was wrong.

"Dr. Rhinehart's plane is missing in the Everglades," Mrs. Sweep told her. Lizzy began to shake. The housekeeper hugged her, and Lizzy buried her head in Mrs. Sweep's arms.

"Oh, he can't be dead," Lizzy cried. "I just saw the most beautiful falling star, and I made a wish that he would come home and stay for a long time."

They went outside and prayed together to the Christian god, to the Seminole gods, to all the gods around the world, and especially to the goddesses of the sea and sky, to protect Dr. Rhinehart wherever he was.

Mrs. Sweep tried to comfort her and kissed her good night, but sleep was out of the question. Lizzy could think only of her father, lost in the Everglades. She *knew* he was alive. She could almost feel that he was trying to talk to her.

She opened the old steamer trunk at the foot of her bed. Inside were presents Lizzy's father had brought her from all over the world: conch pearls from the Bahamas that could only be worn at night, painted coconuts from Tahiti, blankets from New Zealand, puppets from Scotland, and many other exotic things.

She pulled out a very small basket. Four tiny dolls were inside — a family of trouble dolls her father had bought her when they had gone to Guatemala. Legend had it that if you told the dolls your troubles and put them under your pillow, they would solve your troubles while you slept. A name was written on each of their bright little costumes. The father was Julio, the mother was Esmerelda, the young son was Pedro, and the daughter was Maria.

Lizzy went to her bed and placed the trouble dolls on her pillow. Spooner came up beside the bed as Lizzy spoke to the dolls.

"I have a big trouble. My father is missing in the swamps of the Everglades. I need you to help me find him and bring him home safely. My mother has already been taken from me, and I surely need my father."

She kissed them all and put them under her pillow. Then she curled up on her bed and was soon sound asleep with Spooner at her feet.

Later that night she was awakened by noises under her pillow. At first she was frightened, but she took a deep breath and lifted the pillow. To her amazement, she found a busy village of trouble dolls underneath.

She called down to the village, but no one heard her, so she let out a loud whistle and finally got the attention of one trouble doll.

"I'm looking for Julio and his family. They're helping me find my father. Do you know where they are?"

"I'd like to help you," said the trouble doll, "but as you can see, things are very busy here. Many hundreds of years ago when we were first given the power to help, life was simpler. But now the world is so crazy, we are all backed up. I would like to help you find Julio, but I must work on some other troubles right away. Good luck," he finished and tipped his hat as he trotted away.

Lizzy and Spooner searched the busy little world for the dolls. Suddenly Spooner barked, and Lizzy saw Julio and his family under a mango tree by the river.

"Julio," she called. Julio, Esmerelda, Pedro, and Maria all looked up and waved back. "I'm so glad I found you. Any news about my father?"

Julio looked up. "Miss Lizzy," he said, "we have been stuffed away in your trunk and not used until now, so we have never been to the land of trouble dolls. This is our first job, and we are not familiar with all the magic yet."

Little Pedro added, "But we will find your father, Miss Lizzy. We will not stop searching until we do." Maria agreed.

Esmerelda, the kind-looking mother, smiled. She was proud of her little family. "They will do what they say, Miss Lizzy, but I think *you* are the one who has to make a big decision, too. You must come with us to find your father."

Lizzy thought for a moment. "You were given to me as a present by my father, and I truly believe he was telling me to look in the trunk tonight. Now I know why: It was to find you. We'll leave in the morning for the Everglades in my boat, but I need to tell Mrs. Sweep what I'm going to do."

Lizzy waved good night to her new friends and put the pillow back. By now she was so tired from worrying that she didn't even bother to take off her clothes when she crawled under the blanket. Soon she was fast asleep.

She woke up very early to the sound of men talking. Mrs. Sweep was in the kitchen with the sheriff and several Marine Patrol Officers. There had been no news of Dr. Rhinehart, and the weather was going to get bad. A tropical storm had sprung up in the Bahamas and was rapidly moving toward Florida.

The men left, and Lizzy ran in to hug Mrs. Sweep.

"You heard?" the housekeeper asked.

Lizzy nodded. "Mrs. Sweep, do you know about trouble dolls?"
Mrs. Sweep looked down at Lizzy and smiled. She took Lizzy by the
hand, and they walked out to her house. Mrs. Sweep took an old bag off
a hook near her bed and opened it. It was a special bag that held all of
Mrs. Sweep's charms and roots and healing things. She pulled out a
clamshell box and opened it to reveal a family of trouble dolls.

"These are mine, so they can work only for me. I wish I could give
them to you," she said.

"But I have my own! Remember the ones Papa bought for me in
Guatemala? Well, I couldn't sleep last night, and I dug inside my
trunk and brought out the dolls. I remembered the legend he told me,
and I made my wishes and put them under the pillow. I woke up, and a
world of trouble dolls was under my pillow. They told me I had to go
with them to find Papa."

Lizzy was out of breath and a little scared. What would Mrs. Sweep
say? But the old Seminole lady looked down at Lizzy with her wise face.
"Then do what the dolls tell you," she said, "for they carry much magic.
Your father is alive; he was talking to you. Trust your heart and go find
him. But you must hurry."

In less than an hour, Lizzy and Mrs. Sweep were loading supplies
into the *Parakeet.*

"You are in my prayers, little one," the housekeeper whispered.

"Don't worry, Mrs. Sweep," Lizzy said, smiling. "I'm in good hands."

Spooner barked, and Lizzy let go of the boat's bow lines and turned north toward the Everglades. She pulled out a very old map that belonged to her father. Mrs. Sweep had told her it would guide her safely. Lizzy studied it and noticed four small shadows spread across the map. Looking up at her visor, she saw a reflection of the trouble doll family peering down at the map.

"Mind if we have a look?" Julio asked as Mrs. Sweep stood on the dock and waved until the *Parakeet* disappeared over the horizon.

The old woman was not fearful that she had let a nine-year-old girl go off on such a dangerous mission. From past experience, Mrs. Sweep knew the trouble dolls would guide her well and keep her safe.

Lizzy had been out in the bay all her life. From the day her father had given her the *Parakeet,* she had not missed an afternoon cruise. When her father was home, he went with her and pointed out the beauty of nature and the good and bad things people had done to the Florida Keys.

She had a sense of the ocean, but she never had been as far out as she was now. The sheriff had told Mrs. Sweep that Dr. Rhinehart was last heard passing over Panther Point. Though Lizzy could find it on the old map, the entrance to the Everglades would be tricky, and she was counting on help from her little friends. The trouble dolls were still seated on the brim of her visor like lookouts, and Lizzy pointed out the constellation Orion, up where the Jolly Mon and the magic dolphin live. Although it was day, they still shone in the sky as if to guide her.

She found the island of the pink pelicans and decided to stop to rest and have another look at the map.

They put ashore, and the trouble dolls climbed down to examine the map with her. "I see three ways to get in," Julio said. "Do you know which one you will take?" When Lizzy said no, Julio told her, "Here is one way we can help. We look at a map differently than big people do." He winked at Pedro and Maria and said, "Children, see what you can see." With that, the trouble doll children slid down Lizzy's arm and onto the map, where they disappeared.

"Where did they go?" Lizzy asked with a worried look.

"Don't worry," said Julio. "They are in the map. Sometimes it pays to be small."

They were all quietly studying the map when Spooner let out a loud bark. An alligator surfaced near the boat. Esmerelda called to her children, who popped out of the map and dashed for the safety of the visor. Lizzy quieted Spooner and smacked the water with her paddle like her father had taught her, and the alligator swam away. This impressed the trouble dolls very much, and they gave Lizzy a round of applause.

"We found the right channel to take us all the way to Panther Point," Pedro and Maria told her. So the expedition headed upstream.

They saw many more alligators on the banks, and Spooner barked at all of them. Overhead a flock of spoonbills flew north, away from the approaching storm. Lizzy began to realize just how big the Everglades were.

As the sun set in the orange sky, they rounded a bend in the river and came upon an Indian chickee. This would be a good place to spend the night. Lizzy organized the tent, and she and Spooner ate tomato and avocado sandwiches Mrs. Sweep had made for them. Under a star-filled sky, Lizzy said a prayer to protect her father. Then she put the trouble dolls under her pillow in the tent.

"We will bring back good news this time, Miss Lizzy. We are starting to learn our magic." As Lizzy fell asleep, the little people slipped into the trouble doll world. Much work lay ahead of them.

Julio and Esmerelda went back to the village to ask for information, and Pedro and Maria climbed back inside Dr. Rhinehart's map. They met early that morning underneath Lizzy's pillow, and Julio and Esmerelda had exciting news. Some trouble dolls were helping a little girl in Florida to save the manatees from being killed, and they had seen a seaplane near a heart-shaped lake in the Everglades. But Pedro and Maria had seen no such lake in their travels in the map. They woke Lizzy and told her these things.

"That *is* good news, but I don't know how we'll be able to find a heart-shaped lake from ground level." She was worried.

The early morning sky was a bright red to the east, which meant the storm was approaching quickly. Time was running out, and they had to work fast.

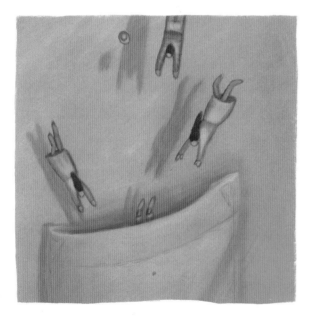

"We could go back and tell Mrs. Sweep the news, and maybe she could get the sheriff to search for the lake with a helicopter," Lizzy said.

"I'm not sure the sheriff would believe our story. Most big people don't believe in us at all," Pedro told her.

"Yes, you're right," Lizzy said quietly. "When I grow up, I'll never be like that. But right now I hardly know what to do, and I need to find my father before the storm hits. I'm scared," she added. Tears filled her eyes.

"Feeling sorry for yourself won't help you find your father," a voice called from a nearby tree. Spooner began to bark at the sky, and the trouble dolls rushed into Lizzy's shirt pocket as she stood up.

"Who's out there?" she asked.

"I'm up here," the voice answered. Lizzy looked up, and in the big magnolia tree she saw a beautiful blue macaw parrot perched on a limb. It was the same bird she had seen the day before.

"You seem to need another pair of eyes from a higher point of view. *I* can find the heart-shaped lake." The big bird spread his wings and glided in a circle toward the ground, landing on the limb of a tree closer to Lizzy. "You can call me Big Blue," the bird told her. "Now put your little friends up here on my neck, and we'll do some flying."

Pedro and Julio looked a bit nervous but climbed aboard Big Blue. The bird squawked and soared off into the sky.

"We'll keep heading for Panther Point," Lizzy shouted to the disappearing parrot.

"Don't worry. I'll find you," Big Blue answered.

The bird flew high and fast, and Julio and Pedro scanned the ground below for the heart-shaped lake. They had flown west to the shores of the Gulf of Mexico and then back east toward the river of grass, when Julio spotted a cockatoo flying toward them.

Big Blue yelled to the cockatoo, "Whitey, do you know where we can find the heart-shaped lake?"

"It's in the middle of Puzzle Bay down on the park border," the cockatoo called back.

"Thanks for the help, mate." Big Blue banked hard toward the park. "We're in luck. I know where we're going now. Natural sense of navigation, lads."

Puzzle Bay was named well, for from the air it was a big circle of bayous, streams, and small lakes — an easy place to get lost. Julio was the first to spot the lake. It was hidden in the middle of many small lakes. Then Big Blue spotted the wrecked plane.

He dove straight for the wreck. Julio and Pedro held on for dear life. Big Blue circled low and finally spotted Dr. Rhinehart in a tree. He was alive but seemed to have a broken leg. How he had made it up the tree was a mystery to Julio and Pedro.

"If *you* were surrounded by alligators, I'm sure you'd find a way, too," Big Blue squawked. "Stay here with the doctor, and I will go find Lizzy. Watch out for the one over there." Julio looked down to see a huge alligator looking up at them.

Lizzy was going as fast as she could toward Panther Point in the *Parakeet* when she spotted Big Blue.

"We've found your father!"

Lizzy let out a big yell of joy, and Spooner barked happily. Maria and Esmerelda jumped up and down on the brim of Lizzy's hat, and Big Blue kept talking. "He's hurt, but Julio and Pedro are taking care of him until we get there," he screeched. Meanwhile Lizzy could feel the wind picking up and knew that the storm was coming faster than anyone had expected. She tuned her little radio in to the weather channel and listened. The forecaster announced that the approaching storm would bring winds of one hundred miles per hour.

"I flew over a short cut," Big Blue squawked. "We should be able to reach him before the storm hits."

Lizzy followed Big Blue down a very narrow channel. At one point the *Parakeet* could barely squeeze through, and Spooner and Lizzy had to get out and walk beside the boat. But finally the little cut emptied into the heart-shaped lake, and on the other side Lizzy could see her father's wrecked plane.

Julio and Pedro shouted at Lizzy to be careful of the alligator, but she fearlessly sped to her father.

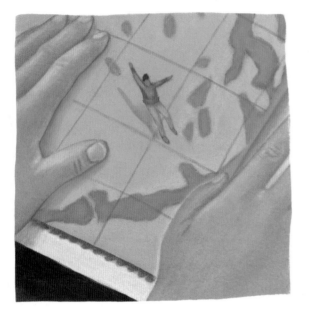

The doctor was very weak, so Lizzy used some lines from her boat to make a sling and lowered her father into the *Parakeet.* She hugged him tightly. Rain was now coming down in sheets, and the wind was blowing hard. "A hurricane is coming," she told her father.

Dr. Rhinehart spoke in a scratchy voice. "There are old Indian caves near Panther Point. Look on the map."

Pedro spoke excitedly. "When I was in the map, I remember seeing some old caves near here. Quick — get the map out, and I will take a look."

Lizzy began to unroll the map, but Pedro jumped in before she could finish. So she went back to take care of her father and made a splint from a tree branch for his leg.

Pedro popped out of the map. "I found the old caves near Panther Point, and I'll guide you."

Big Blue flew off into the storm with Julio and Pedro aboard. According to the radio, the storm was now directly on its way. Lizzy was scared, for her father had fallen asleep and she could barely see in front of her. Esmerelda and Maria were perched on her hat trying to to help when they heard a familiar squawk. It was Big Blue. Lizzy steered the boat toward the sound and finally caught a glimpse of the parrot, Julio, and Pedro. They were soaking wet but had found the cave.

The little expedition edged its way back down the river past Panther Point, and Lizzy slid the boat into the mouth of the cave.

She lit a fire. Dr. Rhinehart looked a little better, and Lizzy fed him some of Mrs. Sweep's chocolate and tea. "I guess this is called growing up in a hurry, Lizzy." He smiled proudly at his daughter.

"I had to smash my way out of the plane before she drifted off. It was awful getting up into that tree, but when I finally got there, I found myself thinking about the time we were in Guatemala. Remember when I bought you those trouble dolls? I could think of nothing else. How odd," he said weakly. Clearly he was in great pain.

"You mean *these* trouble dolls," Lizzy said eagerly. Julio, Pedro, Esmerelda, and Maria were sitting on Spooner's head.

Esmerelda spoke. "I tried to contact both of you after my mother told me about the troubles her keeper, Mrs. Sweep, was having. We had never been used, but we knew we were in the hands of special people. We knew it was time to be of help, and we would not fail."

Dr. Rhinehart was amazed at what he was seeing and hearing but did not argue. "Thank you," he said simply and hugged Lizzy. Spooner trotted over, and they all gathered around the fire.

"And I am the air ambulance service," Big Blue squawked as he landed near them. "Storm turned back to sea. It will be clearing soon."

Dr. Rhinehart looked down at his leg. "I was sitting in the tree out there, and a shooting star passed overhead. I wished so hard that I would see you again. When I thought I was going to die, what I regretted most was not having spent as much time with you as I could. That is going to change, young lady."

"Fine with me," Lizzy said, grinning.

LIZZY WATCHED the sun rise over Florida Bay and thought herself the happiest girl in the world to have her father back at her side. She steered the *Parakeet* toward the dock with Spooner on the bow, stretching into the wind. Lizzy had called Mrs. Sweep on the radio and told her about her father. The doctor, the sheriff, newspaper reporters, and TV people from Miami were waiting on the dock to welcome them home. Lizzy was whistling and singing.

"It's a wonderful day to be alive," Dr. Rhinehart said.

"And a *buenos días, mis amigos,*" Lizzy said as she looked into her pocket, but the trouble dolls had disappeared. She called to Big Blue, who had been perched on the rail of the boat. But he, too, was gone. "I know he'll be back," she thought. It was a good feeling to have such a special friend.

Dr. Rhinehart was taken to the hospital to have his leg set, and the woman on the news from Miami asked Lizzy all kinds of questions about how she had rescued her father.

"I was taught to believe that anything is possible, and I used the gifts my father and my friend, Mrs. Sweep, gave me."

Soon she and Mrs. Sweep were with her father in his hospital room watching the news on TV, and they all looked at each other and smiled. Lizzy hadn't mentioned Pedro, Esmerelda, Julio, Maria, or Big Blue, for they were part of a world the woman on the news would never understand.

When she went to her bedroom that night, Lizzy opened the empty trouble doll basket. Mrs. Sweep came into the room quietly. "They'll be back when you need them," she said.

"But where have they all gone?" Lizzy asked.

Mrs. Sweep came over to her bed and picked up the pillow. There was the trouble doll village, and a big fiesta was being celebrated in honor of Julio, Maria, Esmerelda, and Pedro.

"They are having a party," Lizzy said happily.

"Everyone needs a party," Mrs. Sweep added. She hugged Lizzy, and they put the pillow back. With Spooner at her feet, Lizzy Rhinehart fell asleep knowing she was lucky indeed.